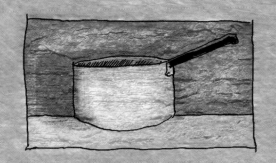

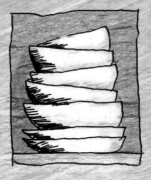

狐狸首先提出，他邀請鶴來吃晚餐⋯
當鶴抵達狐狸的家時，她看到櫃上放置著各式各
樣不同顏色的盤子，大的、高的、矮的、小的。
桌上放著兩隻平底淺碟。

鶴用她那長而薄的鳥嘴往碟上啄食，但不論她怎樣嘗試，
也無法喝到一口湯。

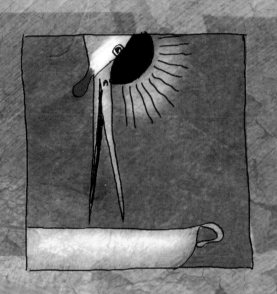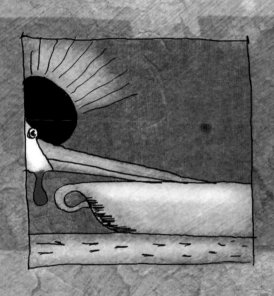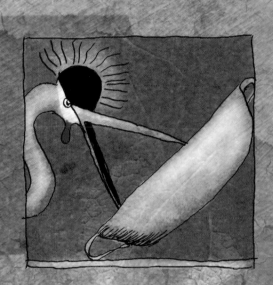

Crane pecked and she picked with her long thin beak. But no matter
how hard she tried she could not get even a sip of the soup.

狐狸與鶴
－ 伊索寓言

The Fox and the Crane
- an Aesop's Fable

retold by Dawn Casey

illustrated by Jago

Traditional Chinese translation by Sylvia Denham

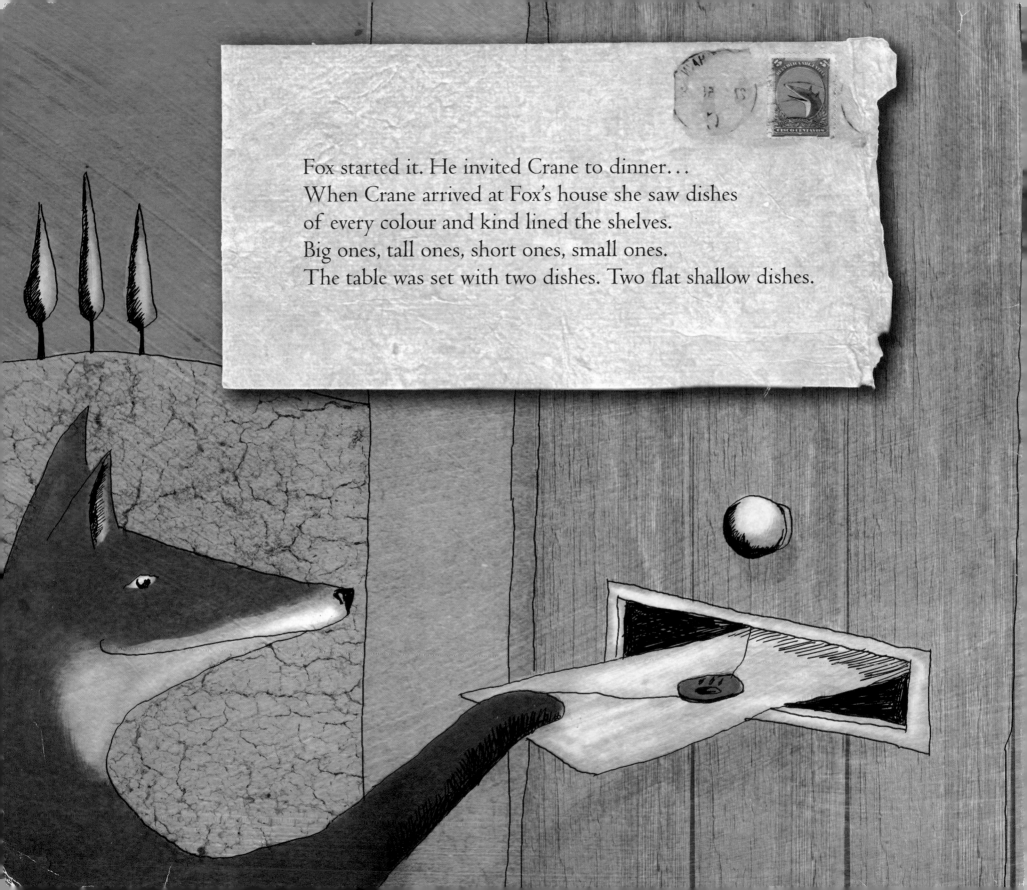

Fox started it. He invited Crane to dinner...
When Crane arrived at Fox's house she saw dishes
of every colour and kind lined the shelves.
Big ones, tall ones, short ones, small ones.
The table was set with two dishes. Two flat shallow dishes.

狐狸一面望著鶴吃力一面竊笑，
他把他的湯送到唇邊，呷呬、
啜吸、咕嘟的將湯都喝乾。
「噯呀！真美味！」他嘲笑說，
並用他的爪背拭抹他的鬍子，
「啊，鶴呀，你還未動過你的湯，」
狐狸假笑著說，「真不好意思，
你不喜歡這湯，」他說道，
並盡量避免輕蔑地笑。

Fox watched Crane struggling and sniggered.
He lifted his own soup to his lips, and with
a SIP, SLOP, SLURP he lapped it all up.
"Ahhhh, delicious!" he scoffed, wiping his
whiskers with the back of his paw.
"Oh Crane, you haven't touched your soup,"
said Fox with a smirk. "I AM sorry you
didn't like it," he added, trying not to snort
with laughter.

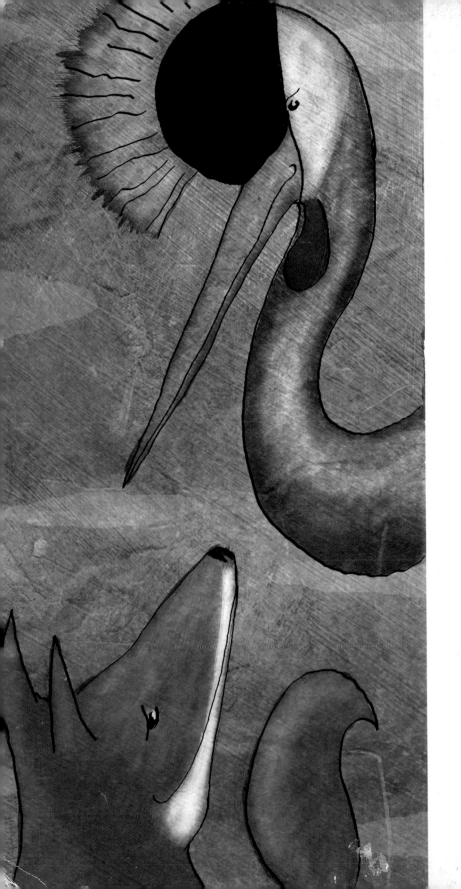

鶴默不作聲，她看看晚餐，又看看碟子，
然後微笑地望著狐狸。
「親愛的狐狸，多謝你的好意，」鶴有
禮貌地說，「請讓我回敬你　－
來我的家吃飯吧。」

當狐狸到達時，窗門大開，一股香味溢出，
狐狸擡高他的鼻子去聞，他的嘴巴垂涎，
肚子隆隆作響，他舐舐他的嘴唇。

Crane said nothing. She looked at the meal. She looked
at the dish. She looked at Fox, and smiled.
"Dear Fox, thank you for your kindness," said Crane
politely. "Please let me repay you – come to dinner at
my house."

When Fox arrived the window was open. A delicious
smell drifted out. Fox lifted his snout and sniffed. His
mouth watered. His stomach rumbled. He licked his lips.

「親愛的狐狸，請進來，」鶴說著，
優雅地展開她的翅膀。
狐狸衝過她，看到櫃上放置著
各式各樣不同顏色的盤子，紅色的、
藍色的、舊的、新的。
桌上放著兩隻盤子，
兩隻高窄的盤子。

"My dear Fox, do come in," said Crane,
extending her wing graciously.
Fox pushed past. He saw dishes of
every colour and kind lined the shelves.
Red ones, blue ones, old ones, new ones.
The table was set with two dishes.
Two tall narrow dishes.

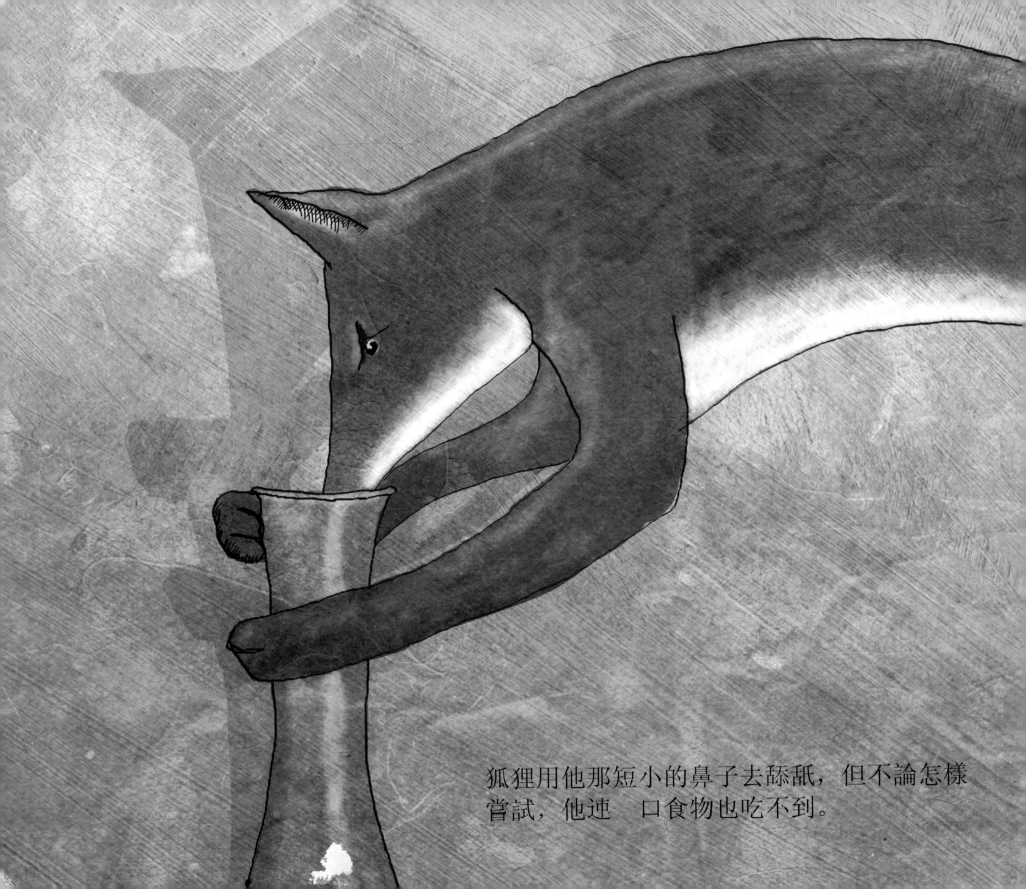

狐狸用他那短小的鼻子去舔舐，但不論怎樣嘗試，他連一口食物也吃不到。

Fox licked and he lapped with his short little snout.
But no matter how hard he tried he could not
get even a mouthful of the meal.

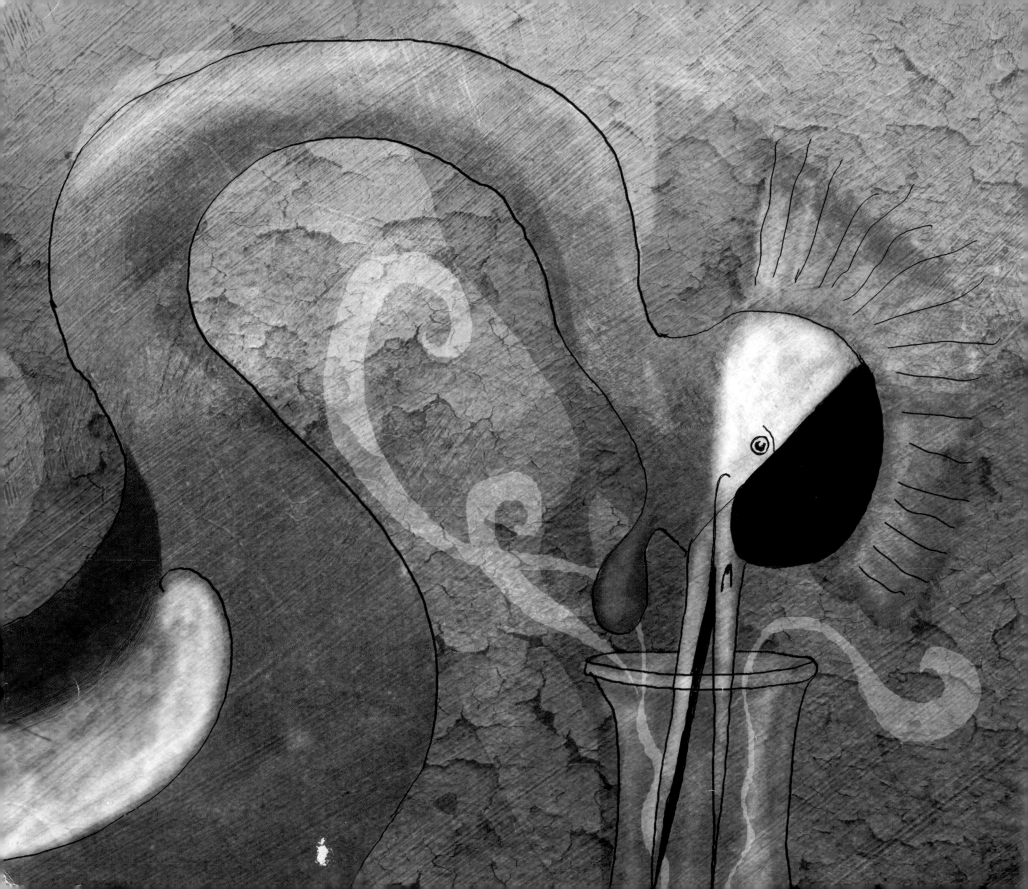

鶴慢慢地吃她的晚餐，細嘗每一口的滋味。
「親愛的狐狸，多謝你到來，」她微笑著說，
「讓我能夠回敬你的好意。」

狐狸的肚子咯咯隆隆地響，當他回家時，他仍然很餓。

Crane ate her meal very slowly, savouring every mouthful.
"Dear Fox, thank you so much for coming," she smiled,
"it has been a pleasure to repay your kindness."

Fox's tummy gurgled and grumbled.
And when he went home, he was still hungry.

The Fox and the Crane

Writing Activity:
Read the story. Explain that we can write our own fable by changing the characters.

Discuss the different animals you could use, bearing in mind what different kinds of dishes they would need! For example, instead of the fox and the crane you could have a tiny mouse and a tall giraffe.

Write an example together as a class, then give the children the opportunity to write their own. Children who need support could be provided with a writing frame.

Art Activity:
Dishes of every colour and kind! Create them from clay, salt dough, play dough… Make them, paint them, decorate them…

Maths Activity:
Provide a variety of vessels: bowls, jugs, vases, mugs… Children can use these to investigate capacity:

Compare the containers and order them from smallest to largest.

Estimate the capacity of each container.

Young children can use non-standard measures e.g. 'about 3 beakers full'.

Check estimates by filling the container with coloured liquid ('soup') or dry lentils.

Older children can use standard measures such as a litre jug, and measure using litres and millilitres. How near were the estimates?

Label each vessel with its capacity.

The King of the Forest

Writing Activity:
Children can write their own fables by changing the setting of this story. Think about what kinds of animals you would find in a different setting. For example how about 'The King of the Arctic' starring an arctic fox and a polar bear!

Storytelling Activity:
Draw a long path down a roll of paper showing the route Fox took through the forest. The children can add their own details, drawing in the various scenes and re-telling the story orally with model animals.

If you are feeling ambitious you could chalk the path onto the playground so that children can act out the story using appropriate noises and movements! (They could even make masks to wear, decorated with feathers, woollen fur, sequin scales etc.)

Music Activity:
Children choose a forest animal. Then select an instrument that will make a sound that matches the way their animal looks and moves. Encourage children to think about musical features such as volume, pitch and rhythm. For example a loud, low, plodding rhythm played on a drum could represent an elephant.

Children perform their animal sounds. Can the class guess the animal?

Children can play their pieces in groups, to create a forest soundscape.

狐假虎威 － 森林之王
－ 中國寓言

The King of the Forest
- a Chinese Fable

retold by Dawn Casey

illustrated by Jago

Traditional Chinese translation
by Sylvia Denham

狐狸正在森林漫步，突然聽到草叢中有東西移動。

抖動 　　　　　　　龐大的東西。

眨動 　　　　　　　黃色的眼睛。

閃動 　　　　　　　像利刀的牙齒。

Fox was walking in the forest when he heard something moving in the long grass.

RUSTLE 　Something big.

BLINK 　Something with yellow eyes.

FLASH 　Something with teeth like knives.

「早晨，小狐狸，」老虎笑著說，嘴裏顯露的都是牙齒。

狐狸吞一口氣。

「真高興見到你，」老虎嗚嗚地說，「我剛剛開始感到肚餓。」

狐狸靈機一觸，「你真大膽！」他說，「你難道不知道我是森林之王嗎？」

「你？森林之王？」老虎說，跟著便大吼地笑。

「如果你不相信我的話，」狐狸威嚴地說，「跟在我的後面走，你便會看到所有人都畏懼我。」

「那我便真要看看了，」老虎說。

於是狐狸漫步橫越森林，老虎得意地在後面跟隨，尾巴提得高高的，直至⋯

"Good morning little fox," Tiger grinned, and his mouth was nothing but teeth.

Fox gulped.

"I am pleased to meet you," Tiger purred. "I was just beginning to feel hungry."

Fox thought fast. "How dare you!" he said. "Don't you know I'm the King of the Forest?"

"You! King of the Forest?" said Tiger, and he roared with laughter.

"If you don't believe me," replied Fox with dignity, "walk behind me and you'll see — everyone is scared of me."

"This I've got to see," said Tiger.

So Fox strolled through the forest. Tiger followed behind proudly, with his tail held high, until…

嘎嘎！
一隻巨大的鉤嘴鷹！但那隻鷹看了老虎一眼便拍
著翅膀飛進叢林裏去。
「看到嗎？」狐狸說，「所有人都畏懼我呢！」
「簡直難以置信！」老虎說。
狐狸繼續在森林漫步，老虎輕輕地在後面跟著，
他的尾巴稍微下垂，直至…

SQUAWK!
A huge hook-beaked hawk! But the hawk took
one look at Tiger and flapped into the trees.
"See?" said Fox. "Everyone is scared of me!"
"Unbelievable!" said Tiger.
　　　　　Fox strode on through the forest.
　　　　　Tiger followed behind lightly,
　　　　　with his tail drooping slightly,
　　　　　until…

咆吼！
一隻大黑熊！但那隻黑熊望了老虎一眼便掉進樹叢中。
「看到嗎？」狐狸說，「所有人都畏懼我呢！」
「簡直難以置信！」老虎說。
狐狸繼續在森林漫步，老虎卑恭地在後面跟著，
他的尾巴在森林的地上拖著，直至⋯

GROWL!
A big black bear! But the bear took one look
at Tiger and crashed into the bushes.
"See?" said Fox. "Everyone is scared of me!"
"Incredible!" said Tiger.
Fox marched on through the forest. Tiger
followed behind meekly, with his tail
dragging on the forest floor, until…

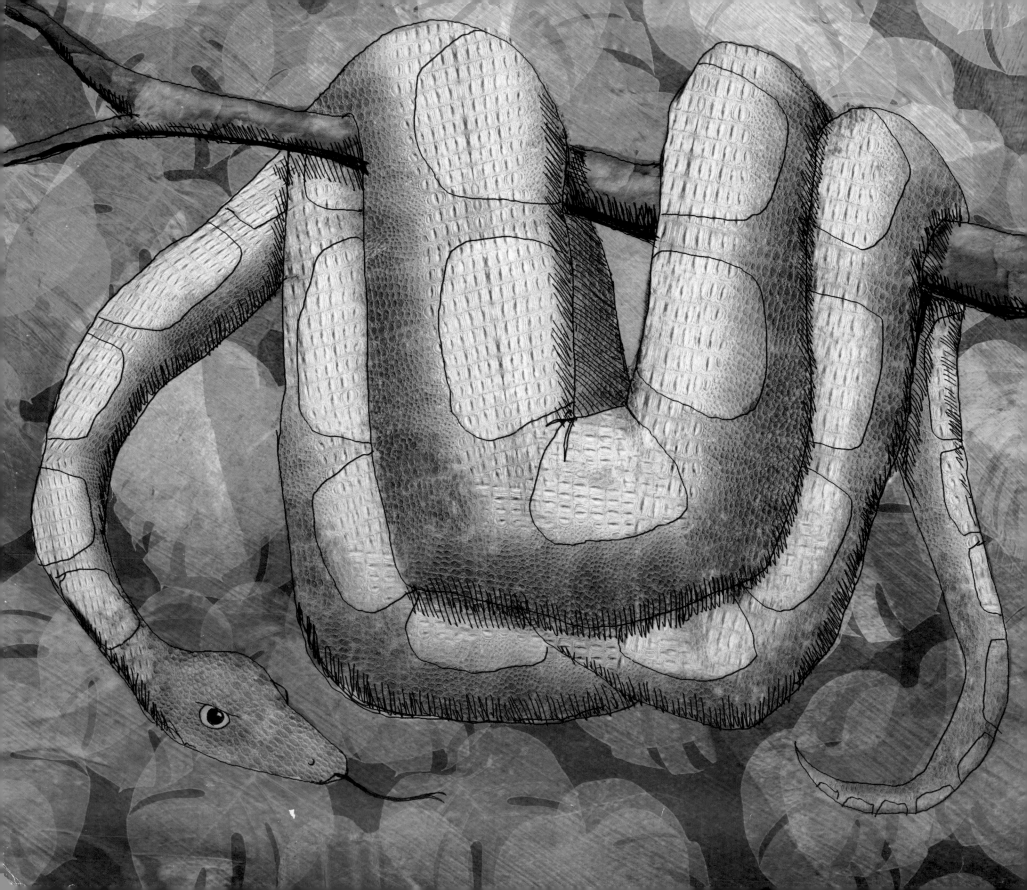

嘶嘶！
一條鬼鬼祟祟溜動著的蛇！但那條蛇望了老虎一
眼便滑行到矮樹叢去。
「看到嗎？」狐狸說，「所有人都畏懼我呢！」

HISSSSSSS!
A slinky slidey snake! But the snake took one look
at Tiger and slithered into the undergrowth.
"SEE?" said Fox. "EVERYONE IS SCARED
OF ME!"

「我看到了，」老虎說，「你是森林之王，而我是你謙卑的隨從。」
「好，」狐狸說，「那麼，你便走吧！」

於是老虎便夾著尾巴畏縮地走了。

"I do see," said Tiger, "you are the King of the Forest and I am your humble servant."
"Good," said Fox. "Then, be gone!"

And Tiger went, with his tail between his legs.

「森林之王，」狐狸對自己笑著說，他的微笑變成咧嘴露齒的笑，咧嘴露齒的笑變成吃吃地笑，狐狸大聲地笑著回家。

"King of the Forest," said Fox to himself with a smile. His smile grew into a grin, and his grin grew into a giggle, and Fox laughed out loud all the way home.

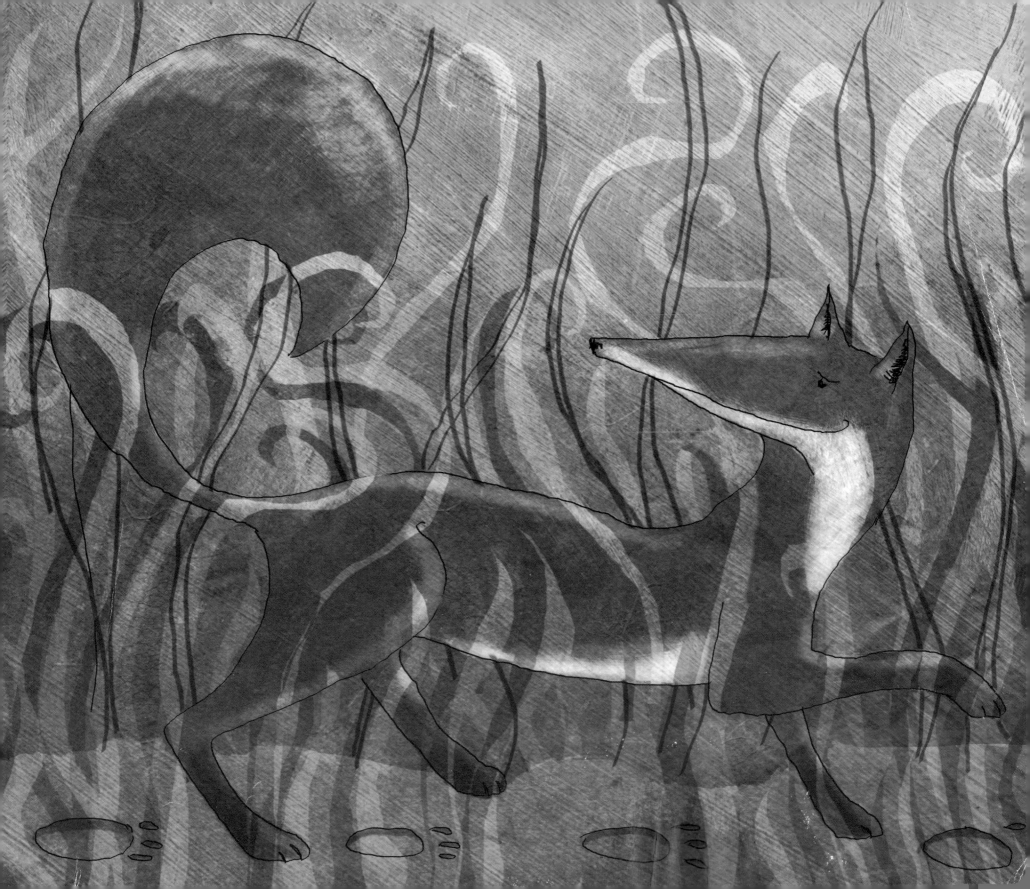

To my Nana, with love ~ DC
For my wife, Alex ~ J

First published in 2006 by Mantra Lingua Ltd
Global House, 303 Ballards Lane
London N12 8NP
www.mantralingua.com

A CIP record for this book is available from the British Library